MURDER FOR HIRE

BY JACK KING

Special thanks to Keith Scarborough and Masterpiece Printing.

Special recognition to Kevin Gilmore for Graphics and Cover Art.

Contents

This is a true story; my father was murdered, so this book was written as fiction for legal purposes.

The names, relationships and locations have been changed to protect the innocent and the guilty.

Any similarity in locations or names is purely a coincidence and in no way is it meant to incriminate or insinuate the real circumstances.

MURDER FOR HIRE

CHAPTER ONE: THE PHONE CALL

MURDER FOR HIRE

CHAPTER ONE: THE PHONE CALL

It was Wednesday night, February 5th, cold and snowing in Oklahoma City.

My wife and I had just finished supper and the kids were about to go to bed.
I was watching television and the phone rang. It was my mother, her voice was frantic "Jack Charles, your dad got a phone call around nine o'clock, that said they were the security patrol for the business and the back door had been left unlocked. They needed him to come and make sure nothing had been stolen and secure the premises. Your dad has been gone for over an hour and I can't get him to answer the phone. Would you go down and check on him?" I said, "Sure, but don't worry, everything is fine." It was a little before 11pm.
My dad's business was just about 6 minutes from our home. I wasn't that sure

everything was fine, so I took a pistol with me, just in case everything was not fine.

When I pulled up behind the business, my dad's blue pick-up truck was running, the headlights were on and the driver's door was open. With that setting, my first thought was, he must have just gone back into the business for something. You don't leave your door open on your car unless you are just going to be a minute. I noticed his .22 caliber rifle was in the gun rack inside the cab. He kept it there for the weekends when he went to his farm. He would often shoot snakes.

As I approached the back door to the business, I noticed his keys were still in the lock, another sign that he must have just gone back in for a minute, leaving his keys in the door.

I pushed the door open and stepped into a dark hallway and yelled "DAD!"

Silence.
I yelled again, "DAD!"

Nothing.

I walked down the darkened hallway a few more feet and noticed an exit light on at the end of a hallway to my right. It was then that I saw my dad laying face down on the floor. He looked like he was unconscious. There were no visible signs of blood so I bent down to feel his neck and see if there was a pulse.

Nothing.

I turned his body over and realized he had been shot in the head twice and in the chest once. At that moment I did what I think any son would do.

I pulled his body up to my chest and made a vow to him that I would avenge his death and bring his murderer to justice.
Then I looked to heaven and said, " God, why did you let this happen?"

My mom had called the police right after she called me. She didn't stay home like I asked, she came to the business and arrived right after the police arrived, but they wouldn't let her see dad.

My mind was swirling and exploding with questions. My background as a former Drill Sergeant in the United States Army caused me to want to take charge and begin the pursuit of my father's murderer instantly. But when I saw my mother, we both were overwhelmed with emotion.

"There's such a deep pain and ache in my heart. What causes that? How do I make it go away?"

Her husband was dead.
My father was dead.

I'm not sure how long we held each other and wept, deep, hard sobbing. It seemed like it wouldn't stop. This can't be happening! There's such a deep pain and ache in my heart. What causes that? How do I make it go away? I told the first police officer that my uncle, my mom's brother, was a Lieutenant with the police department. As soon as he arrived he took my mother into his car.

I turned around to the first officer that arrived on the scene and said." Where's the security patrol?

He said, "What do you mean?" I told him about the phone call my dad received around 9pm from the security patrol.

It was close to 11pm when I got to the murder scene and there was no security patrol.

Now it was an hour later and still no security patrol. Somebody needs to find the security patrol. Where did they go? Why did they leave?

The officer asked me if I knew the name of the company that patrolled the business. I asked mom and she didn't know. I told them my father's partner would know.

The officer and I went over to his car and radioed his dispatcher and asked them to call the partner, Barry Tindale.

We could hear the dispatcher dialing the number and could hear Mrs. Tindale answer the phone. "Is Barry Tindale there?"

She said, "Yes, he just walked in the house."

I didn't realize how crucial that statement would be later in the investigation.

Barry came to the phone; the dispatcher identified himself and informed him that his partner had been found dead at their business. Barry said, "Really?" The policeman said, "Yes, we need you to come down to the office. We also need to know who your security company is that patrols the business."

" Overnight Security," he responded. "We need that number, quick" the officer said.

Once he provided it, the police called and found out it was not them that placed the call to my father.

The policeman asked the security company how often they patrolled the business each night.

Their response was once an hour.

I was furious. "Once an hour? My dad went to his office around 9pm; I got there a little before 11pm.

It's now after midnight and they haven't driven by yet? What kind of half-baked, irresponsible security company is this?

Get the head of the security patrol company out of bed and get his rear end down here!

I want some answers!"

Then who was it that called?

Someone called my dad at home and said they were the security patrol to lure him to the office. Oh no, someone set him up.

"SOMEBODY IS GOING TO PAY FOR THIS!"

MURDER FOR HIRE

CHAPTER TWO: Why The Attorney?

MURDER FOR HIRE

CHAPTER TWO: Why The Attorney?

There were so many policemen, detectives, and neighbors from the neighborhood around the business trying to find out what happened.
I could hear them.

Someone dead?

A burglary?

How was he killed?

Are we in danger?

Is the murderer still on the loose?

Was it an argument?

The police couldn't tell if anything was missing from the business. They did know this. It wasn't a surprised burglar.

When my dad's partner arrived, he had an attorney with him.

I said, "Why the attorney?" He did not respond.

The entire atmosphere of wondering if it was a burglary, robbery or what, now changed to the suspicion of a murder.
The police began to ask Barry questions. Where were you tonight? He said he got home around seven pm.
What about customers or clients that might have a reason to lure your partner to murder him?
What about anyone in his personal life? Barry kept looking at his attorney to see if he should answer each question before he would respond to the policeman.
One thing Barry did volunteer. He asked if my dad had any money on him when they found him. The policeman said yes, he did. Barry said, " I gave him $5000 cash earlier today to deposit in our payroll account."

The policeman said, "He didn't have near that much on him, just $38.

It sounded fishy to me.

I didn't understand any of this. They were partners for eleven years. Why does he feel he needs an attorney?

The police detectives asked if they could come to our house, since it was so close to the offices and finish questioning my mother and I. It wasn't too long after we arrived at my home that, Marilyn Tindale, the wife of my dads' partner arrived.

As I came down the hall I saw her leaning against the bedroom door with her ear against it trying to listen to the investigators.

I told her to get out of my house; she was not welcome and to never come back. I was still perturbed that dad's partner came to the murder scene with an attorney.

> *"I realized my entire wealth of knowledge about murder cases was based on two things; television and newspapers."*

I began to piece things together from the last few hours and realized that dad's partner, very well could have been the one who killed him or hired someone to do the killing for him.

I sat there and began to think about what I knew about a murder investigation and realized my entire wealth of knowledge about murder cases was based on two things; television and newspapers. Most of those get solved and they get solved quickly. On television, cases are solved in one or two hours.

But, unless one has experienced such a tragedy, how do you know what to expect? I was not ready for anything less than total vindication. I wasn't ready for bureaucratic slow downs or lackadaisical attitudes or poor work habits from anyone, especially, detectives or attorneys. I knew I would need to help keep things going.

We were up most the night. I'm not sure when or if I went to sleep that night.

But my last thought that night was the vow I made to my father. I will avenge your death!

The next morning, Thursday, the police were shocked to find that his partner had cleaned up the blood and was having business as usual.

Partners for eleven years, how does that work?
No remorse? No respect?

I was upset that he was allowed to go back into the business before the homicide investigators had cleared the scene much less clean it up and go on as if nothing ever happened. I headed to the police headquarters to see my uncle who was a Lieutenant. He took me to the homicide division and introduced me to the Senior Homicide investigator, Ray Hart, who in-turn introduced me to the detective, Terry Jordan, that would be in charge of dad's case.

We sat and discussed every thing I could think of that I knew about my dad and his business, his relationship with his partner, and the business dealings he was having a few weeks before he was going to sell his part of the business.

My dad and I had just started to really talk and confide with each other.
It wasn't until I got married and had children that my dad and I began to talk as men.
All of a sudden it seemed like we had so much in common as we would meet for a drink before going home and talk about things, bills, kids, wife stuff.
Dad had told me his partner was not able to explain to him why they weren't making a profit and their cash flow was not what it should be. It was causing him to have to hold his payroll checks before he could deposit them. My dad was a great salesman for the business and sales were up. It just did not make sense that the cash flow was as bad as it was.

But his partner was the accountant and he could not explain a legitimate reason for the financial problems in a way that Dad could understand.

My dad was finally at the point where he was going to offer his partner the buyout agreement or right of first refusal. In other words, if Dad found a buyer and got an offer to sell his part of the partnership, then Barry would have the first right to refuse that offer and buy it himself for the same price offered.

The only problem with that for Barry is the potential buyer would bring in their own accounting people or auditors and would totally reveal any discrepancies in the accounting procedures or possibly discover any fraud that was taking place or any cover up of misused or misplaced funds.

My dad didn't know what was wrong, he just wanted out.

Dad had begun to talk to me about us going into business together. I guess I was too full of pride to accept this because I wanted to prove to him I could make it on my own without his help.

What is up with that? Why do so many sons not want their father's help?

I'm not sure why I didn't want to join him in business. I guess every son wants to prove to his father, he can make it on his own.
I knew this; I would never get to show my father I could make it.
I guess it's the little boy in each one of us wanting to have our father's approval. We want to hear him and see him in the stands being proud and saying, "That's my boy!"
Even as a grown man, I would love to hear those words from my Dad. Good job son!
That couldn't happen now.
I would prove one thing. I would keep my word and the vow I made.

Somebody is going to pay for this!

MURDER FOR HIRE

CHAPTER THREE: The Funeral

MURDER FOR HIRE

CHAPTER THREE: The Funeral

It's amazing how, in one moment of time your entire life is changed by a tragedy. Someone else's decision changes your course in life, changes the way you think and live. It proves that decisions never affect just the person making the decision.

I had not realized the responsibilities that came with being the oldest son. Everyone kept looking to me for answers. It was as if I was now expected to be the father.

I do know one thing. Nothing else mattered. I would get the answers.

This was the first thing I thought about in the morning. It's what I thought about all day long and the last thing I thought about at night.

I had to deal with things I had never faced before. I'm not sure what the most difficult thing was I had to deal with.

It all hurt. It all had a deeper degree of pain. I had never experienced such grief. I tried to sort out what hurt the most.

Seeing my mother that first moment at the murder scene?

Seeing my dad lying there dead?

Or was it when I had to tell my brothers and sister?

Or was it going to my dad's father and telling him.

How do you measure hurt or pain? That deep ache inside my chest seemed to go deeper and deeper each time I had to tell someone else. I wasn't sure I could tell one more person.

Then it hit me. My dad's father, Pappy, didn't know what had happened.
This was too overwhelming. Pappy was old and frail. How would it affect him?

Was his heart strong enough?

I didn't know him as well as I knew my grandfather on my mom's side.
I lost my maternal grandfather when I was ten. My middle name, Charles, was his first name. I loved being with him. We spent a lot of time together.
He was so funny, actually more ornery than funny, but at ten years old, things he did and said were always funny.
Pappy lived in Arkansas and we didn't get to spend as much time together so I wasn't sure how it would go or if I would be able to hold up emotionally.

My drill sergeant background should help. It was always a mentality of, take names, kick butt and ask questions later, just get the job done.

This was a job I didn't want!

You would think I could be strong in this. Does being strong just mean, you don't cry? Why is crying construed as weakness for a man in society?

I guess I wasn't as strong as I thought, because when I walked into his antique store, I broke and began to weep and tried to tell him dad was gone, shot, dead,

> "A grandson should never have to tell a grandfather that his son has died."

murdered.
He already knew something bad was wrong. I was there by myself without mom and dad.

It was devastating for him and devastating for me.

A grandson should never have to tell a grandfather that his son has died. It's unnatural, because the younger is not supposed to die before the older.

My drive back was filled with the full gambit of emotions. This all seemed so unfair. I needed to be with my wife and children. I needed to be there for my younger brothers, my older sister and, most of all, my mother. I couldn't be everything to everybody.

There were so many unanswered questions.
My biggest question was, why did you let this happen God?

My mind was on the investigation and not the funeral arrangements.

The day of the funeral was total numbness.

My mom was like a zombie. The doctor had heavily sedated her.
Funerals are to bring closure, recognize and cherish all the good of the relationship you had with the deceased.

This wasn't going to happen because of the circumstances. Especially the fact that Barry and Marilyn Tindale were there acting like they were sorrowful. They got there late and left early.

I didn't want them there at all and it was all I could do to tolerate them, much less keep from acting on my anger.

I couldn't believe this had happened. I wanted to wake up and realize it's all a dream.

It was no dream! The last viewing of my father in his casket was not the last memory I wanted of him.

The funeral home had done as good as they could to make my dad's face look like him. But it didn't.

It hurt more and made me angrier.

Relatives, friends and business associates from all over the United States had been calling for days. They began to arrive outside the church and all eyes were focused on us as we went into the pastor's study. Everyone was so compassionate and thoughtful. So many great memories attached to each person. I wanted our family to be able to mourn and grieve our loss and honor our Dad. This wasn't happening.

Everyone kept saying, "Jack you're being so strong for your mother."
My translation of that was based on something my father had instilled in me.
Big boys don't cry. Be strong, don't cry.
It was something that would be dealt with years later in my life.
That's why the drive back from Pappy's was so emotional.

I had anger I didn't know I had.
I had hate I didn't know I had.
I had revenge I didn't know I had.
I had pain in my heart I had never known before.
I did have one other thought. . How can I get a permit to carry a gun?

They are not going to get away with this. Somebody is going to pay for what they did!

MURDER FOR HIRE

CHAPTER FOUR: THE INVESTIGATION

MURDER FOR HIRE

CHAPTER FOUR: THE INVESTIGATION

The detectives found very little evidence at the murder scene. There were no forcible signs of entry. How did the killer get inside the building? Who let him inside? With the position of my father's body and the direction the bullets entered his body, the shooter had to already be inside the building waiting. Meaning they were let in or had a key.

There were three rounds fired into my dad, one in the heart and two in the head after he was on the floor were recovered. The one that went through his heart was recovered in a wall behind where my father entered the hallway. The other two rounds were recovered from under my dad's head as he was shot twice in the head while lying on the floor. They were both badly damaged and almost flattened from hitting the concrete floor. The detectives realized it would be extremely difficult to get a match on the gun they were fired from. The decision had to be made of whether to send them to the Federal Crime Lab or the State Bureau of Investigation.

The State Crime Lab would be quicker but they didn't have the same sophisticated equipment and manpower as the Federal Lab. The Federal Lab could take eight or nine months.

The detectives reminded me that they only had one shot at convicting the murderer and they had to have an iron clad case and evidence for that to happen.

Even though it would take longer, it was better to have the Federal Lab run the tests. So the rounds from the killers' gun were sent to the Federal Bureau of Investigation's ballistics lab.

I began to realize if it took eight or nine months to get the results back then it could possibly be a year or so before any charges were filed or a trial was held.

I never thought, as each day would pass that this could drag out for a year or more before it was solved.

I had to stay involved closely with every aspect of the investigation because there were so many other homicide cases; sometimes they seemed to ignore my dad's case.

I was at the police station everyday when the detectives' shift began at 7am.

Something interesting surfaced that first morning while I was at the police station.

Two days after my father was killed, the bank called my mom. Dad's payroll check had bounced. The bank manager told mom that had never happened before. She assured my mother that no checks would be returned for insufficient funds. My mom knew that Dad and his partner would have to hold their paychecks occasionally, due to cash flow.

One thing I knew about my dad; returned checks were an abomination to him.

I told Terry Jordan, the lead detective on my dad's case. He called Barry, my dad's partner and asked him what was going on, since payroll checks were bouncing.
Barry said that he had given my dad five thousand dollars cash to deposit in the payroll account on Wednesday, to cover the rest of the payroll. That's the day my dad was murdered. We found out that was not the normal procedure. Money was normally transferred from the operating account to the payroll account.
The money was never deposited. Barry informed the police that my father must have still had the cash on him when he was murdered and the murderer took it, thus the motive for the murder.
Yeah, right.

I knew none of this made sense.

If my father actually had been given the cash to deposit in order to cover his payroll check and others, then he would have deposited it.

My dad deposited his paycheck on Wednesday, the day he was murdered. He wouldn't have deposited it if he didn't think the money was in the payroll to cover it. No way, absolutely not, I knew my dad.

I told Terry, this bucket is not holding water.

Barry is trying to cover up the five thousand dollars. He didn't give my dad the money, because if that were true, he would have deposited the cash, and then deposited his paycheck knowing there was enough in the account.

Since that did not happen, then dad deposited his check based on Barry telling him the money was there, knowing dad would be dead and wouldn't be able to speak about what really happened. This very scenario made me realize, Barry had planned this whole thing and was the mastermind if not the perpetrator. This piece of the puzzle would fit in later.

They had so many questions about my fathers' habits and patterns. Who might have had it in for my dad? What else was he involved in? Could this be from a jealous husband? A disgruntled employee? A vendor that was owed money? Or was his partner about to be exposed?

Every question and avenue had to be pursued and investigated.
The Senior Homicide investigator, Roy Hart, told me, "Jack, there's the real possibility your dad's case may never be solved." I said, "No We're going to find who did this or who was responsible. It was at the moment I realized I would not let up or let them ease up on my father's case.
It was almost 3pm and they said their shift was over. Your shift is over? We're just getting started and you're going home? Who is going to work on this on the night shift? They said it had not been assigned yet.

> "Jack, there's the real possibility your dad's case may never be solved."

The detective stopped me and said, "Jack, this may be your life now but it's just our job, not our life." We have family and other things in our lives after we get off work each day. It was a truth I didn't want to hear or deal with right now.

I decided to stay and make sure they assigned my dad's case to someone on the evening shift (3pm to 11pm) and the graveyard shift (11pm to 7am).
I saw one of my high school classmates, David Stewart come in the homicide division who now worked for the police force. As we talked, we began to count the guys we went to high school that also worked at the police department.

He said if there is anything we can do to help with your family or the investigation, let us know. The senior homicide investigator took him up on that.
He asked all those who were willing, to give some of their personal time to canvas the neighborhood within a five block area

of the business. He thought there might be someone that heard or saw something unusual the night of the murder. Friends of mine went house-to-house, business-to-business, knocking on doors informing residents and owners about the tragedy. Asking every person if there was anything unusual about that night they remembered. They knocked on doors at close to a hundred homes and businesses.

It paid off.

David Stewart was one of the first to go out in the community on his own time. He reaped results immediately.

One young teenager, a girl fifteen years old said something unusual did happen to her and her friend the night of February 5th.

They were at the Silver Castle Café around 9pm and had decided to walk home in time to see the ten o'clock news. Her boyfriend had been arrested earlier in the day and she wanted to see if it was on the news. Their path took them across the back parking lot of my father's business. They noticed a station wagon parked with the drivers' window down and a man sitting in the drivers seat with his arms and head leaning on the steering wheel. The two girls were talking as they walked by the drivers' side of the car. The man looked up at them, and then quickly put his head back down on the top of the steering wheel, between his arms, as if he didn't want them to see his face.

David asked her if she and her friend would be willing to come to the police station and try to identify the man from police photos. She agreed and gave them her friend's information.

He immediately called Terry Jordan, the homicide detective, to let him know what had surfaced.

Terry called me and said, "We found some witnesses that saw a man sitting in his car behind your dad's business close to the time your dad got the phone call."

The girls were scheduled to view pictures at the police department at the same time, same day in separate rooms.

When shown a picture of Barry Tindale, each girl identified him as the man sitting in the car, waiting on my father. This was huge! But it got better, there was more.

Another friend on the force, Kelly Sanchez, came across a guy at a local bakery that he had previously arrested on some drug charges. The policeman asked him if he knew about the shooting a few weeks earlier. He didn't know about this particular shooting but said that someone had contacted him about what it would cost to have a contract put on someone. He told the man $5000, but he was only into burglaries not hard crime like murder. They wanted him to come to the police station to look over some pictures. He said he would but he wanted a favor for a lesser charge on a case he had pending.

They told him his information would have to be critical in making an arrest and testifying at the trial.
He agreed and came to the station.

Bingo! Same identification. Barry Tindale!

Amazing how satisfying and fulfilling this was to me.

Now I knew I had to have a private investigators license, especially, to carry a gun.
Daily, I would update my family on the investigation.
This was a day that was full of encouragement. We were on the right trail, finally.

 Someone is going to pay for murdering my dad!

MURDER FOR HIRE

CHAPTER FIVE: The Pursuit

MURDER FOR HIRE

CHAPTER FIVE: The Pursuit

I needed to be able to have the same parameters and access as the police had to the investigation. The detective department recognized the importance of my involvement as they progressed in the investigation.

It seemed as if I was the only one that could see the whole picture or put the pieces together.

I'm not bragging but they certainly didn't have the same level of intensity and tenacity that I had, to pursue my father's case.
I wanted to make sure every shift had someone assigned to the case and were addressing it on a weekly if not daily basis.
Terry Jordan informed me no other shift would have the case as high a priority since he was the lead on dad's case. But he

would make sure they followed his leads so progress would be made shift to shift.

I still didn't believe in my heart that they could or would pursue it like I expected.

I had no idea it would take so long to bring things together for justice to be served.

I went through all the procedures to become a licensed private investigator thus allowing me to have a permit to carry a gun.

I didn't want one gun, I wanted two guns.

I bought two Smith & Wesson, nine millimeter, with special 11 round clips and shoulder holsters. I had been trained in the Army with a 45 caliber automatic and was an expert marksman. These two weapons were so much sweeter.

Amazing how confident it made me feel, even though it was a false confidence, as I would realize later.

I began to go out on my own to all the places my dad frequented or called on in his business.

One question the detective asked me was could this be a jealous husband that shot my father. And did I know whether my dad's marriage was solid or could he have been fooling around with another man's wife. I assumed everything was fine with my mom and dad, since they argued like most husbands and wives.

My dad was an extremely hardworking man. He worked two jobs most his life to provide for us.

But it did raise questions in my mind and I decided to pursue it.

After months of going to some of his former customers I ended up at the Quality Motel, which was right up the street from where my mom and dad lived.
There was a club inside and was a place my dad and I would meet for a drink before we headed home at the end of the day. The club was also a business account for my dad's business and he would check on their supplies to see if they needed anything. I walked inside and the manager, Donna Miller, immediately came over to

me and hugged me and began to say how sorry she was for what had happened to my father. I sat down and asked her the question. Was my father ever in here with another woman? Donna raised her eyebrows and said, "No way, not your dad, never!" It was reassuring to see how adamant she was about that.

She looked at me and said, "There was someone else in here the night before your father was murdered and he met with someone staying at the motel. I said, "Really? Who was it?" She said, "Your dad's partner Barry Tindale." She said he introduced her to the man he was meeting and she wrote the man's name down on the bar tab. At the time, she said if the guy came back in the bar she could call him by his first name and the more personable she was the better tip she got.

She wasn't sure if it meant anything or was significant in the investigation but she said the guy staying at the hotel was not the normal businessman you would expect a business owner to be associating with and it seemed weird and they both seemed uncomfortable. I asked Donna if she still had the bar tab and she said yes. She went into the back room for a while and came out with the tab. It had the name, " Jack Steele" written in the top corner. She suggested I might go to the night clerk in the motel and tell him what happened to my father and offer him $20 to see the man's registration form. So that's exactly what I did.

The young man was a college student and seemed impacted by my story and wanted to help in any way he could. He went to the registrations for Feb 4th and pulled the bill out. I looked at it and wrote down everything, Jack Steele, 15 Burwyck Drive, Akron, OH.

Special comments said, "Requests room on west side of motel' and he paid with cash. The bill also had two other charges on it. One for $4.19 and one for $5.68 and these letters beside each amount, "ldph" I asked what they meant. The clerk said, "long distance phone calls, I have the numbers that were called if you want them." I said, "You betcha."

I went to a phone and called information in Akron Ohio. I asked for the phone number for Jack Steele. She said she had several Jack Steele's listed. I gave her the address and she said none of them were listed with that address.

I felt like I had no choice but to tell what had happened. When she heard my father had been found dead, she wanted to do whatever she could to help, even though she sounded like she really wasn't suppose to search for phone numbers based on addresses. When I gave her the address, she said that address and phone number was listed to an Earl and Ethel Brown. So I asked her for the phone number. When I called the number an older lady answered the phone.

I identified my self and began to tell her my situation, knowing she would have no idea who I was or what happened.

But when I said this is Jack King, she interrupted me and said, "Oh My God Jack, we're so sorry about your dad."

I was stunned. I said, "Wait, how do you know about my dad?" She said, "Barry Tindale is our son-in-law; Marilyn is our daughter, she called and told us what happened."

It's hard to describe what my thoughts were, much less my gambit of emotions. I knew I had to act normal and get off the phone. I didn't tell why I was calling. I thanked her and hung up.

I almost felt sorry for her and her husband that Barry had possibly involved them by using their address. It didn't make sense. It seemed too good to be true. It seemed really stupid. Why would you use your mother- in –law's address on a registration of someone who didn't live at that address? I had a humorous thought as I asked myself that question; maybe Barry used her address intentionally because it was his mother-in-law.

I couldn't wait to call Sgt Jordan.

When he answered his phone, I asked him if he was sitting down. I explained everything that happened at the club with Donna Miller and the clerk, distance in Ohio night the long operator and the

> "My dad would get adamant and furious when it came to insufficient checks."

phone call to the Brown's. He said that's unreal that Barry would be so stupid to use his in-laws address on a fake registration. I again joked about it and said maybe he's trying to get back at his in-laws.

I told Terry they must have made up the Jack Steele name to try and throw everyone off the trail if it was ever uncovered. Terry said, "Maybe not." I asked, why? He said that he found out from an employee at the business that there was a Jack Steele that owed the company about $16,000 from an insufficient check for supplies and services rendered.

I remembered my dad telling me about the situation but I had no idea the guys name was Jack Steele. This did reemphasize the point I had made earlier in the case about returned checks. My dad would get adamant and furious when it came to insufficient checks. For someone to owe that much was significant. I could just imagine what my dad did and said to this Jack Steele. Actually this Steel guy had done nothing to try and make the check good. I later found out from my mom that dad had threatened him with all types of legal pursuit and other ramifications that would ruin Steele's business if he didn't make the check good.

When my mom would mess up in her checkbook and have returned checks my dad would get so upset with her. I can imagine how upset he would get over a $16,000 hot check!

I had to find this Jack Steele to talk to him. Terry told me it would be best if he talked to him in an official capacity. As bad as I wanted a face-to-face confrontation, I was inclined to agree.

In the meantime, Terry was contacting the Kansas Bureau of Investigation to have them run the phone numbers listed on this Jack Steele's hotel bill and question the parties to whom those numbered belonged.

Finally, we're getting somewhere.

Somebody is definitely going to pay for this!

MURDER FOR HIRE

CHAPTER SIX: The Mistresses

MURDER FOR HIRE

CHAPTER SIX: The Mistresses

Both phone numbers the Kansas Bureau of Investigation contacted were in small Kansas towns not too far from Wichita.

A KBI agent called the first number and explained they were investigating the murder of a businessman in Oklahoma. A man registered under the name of Jack Steele called your phone number on February 4th at 4:00pm from a hotel in Oklahoma. The lady said she didn't know anyone by that name. The agent pressed her for who could have been the one to take the call and talk for over 15 minutes.

She said no one else except her husband lived there and he doesn't get home from work until after 6pm. He pressed some more to think whether she had talked to anyone from out of state, long distance.

She finally broke down crying and admitted she did talk to someone who was in Oklahoma for a day or two. But his name was not Jack Steele, but John Blake.

The agent asked for all the details of the conversation and how to find him and what her relationship was to this man. She said she was having an affair with this man whenever he came through Kansas. He was calling to tell her he wouldn't be able to see her on this trip because he was repossessing cars. It was a big job for him because it would generate about $5000.

She said she didn't have a current phone number or an address for him, because he was moving to Canada. He always called her from whatever motel where he was staying. She said he did a variety of things to make money, mostly repossess cars.

She begged the agent to not include her husband in the questioning because he didn't know anything about this man or their relationship. The agent explained in a murder investigation that every person involved could be subpoenaed.

They would have to get a signed affidavit from her for their files. He said he was sorry, but it may be best to tell her husband now, rather than later if she was summoned. The agent made her aware of the consequences of hindering an investigation and for aiding and abetting a suspect now that she was aware of the homicide investigation.
He left her his contact information and informed her to let him know when this John Blake called her again.

The agent placed a call to the second number from the motel registration.

Again a lady answered the phone and he explained they were investigating the murder of a businessman in Oklahoma. And a man registered under the name of Jack Steele called their phone number on February 4th at 4:30pm from a hotel in

Oklahoma. The lady said she didn't know anyone by that name.

He asked her if she knew a John Blake and she said yes. The agent told her he needed to know all the details of their conversation and how to find him and what her relationship was to this man and when the last time she heard from him.

She said her relationship was personal. The agent asked her if she was married. She said yes. He was stunned that this John Blake was having affairs with two different married women in two towns just a few miles apart.

The woman then told the agent that John Blake had called her a few months earlier from the Canadian border and needed to mail some things for her to keep. She said she still had the package but no idea what it contained.

The agent said they would be sending a local police officer to her house to pick up the package.

She said the call on February 4th was to tell her he wouldn't be able to see her on this trip because he was repossessing cars. It was a big job for him because it would generate about $5000. It was interesting that he wanted both his mistresses to know he was making big money on this trip.

The agent explained the same thing to this woman that he had explained to the other woman about the affidavit and a possible subpoena to appear in court should this become a trial case. This information created several questions for the agent.

First, the contents of the package; what did he have at the Canadian border that he could not take into their country?

Second, what did this John Blake really do for a living? The agent typed a full report of what he had uncovered so far from the two phone calls and sent it to Sgt. Jordan in Oklahoma City.

Now they had a name, John Blake, to run through the computer system for warrants. We could find out who John Blake really was. He got responses from three different cities.

The first information contained the city where he was born, Oklahoma City. The second city was Phoenix where he was wanted for extortion. The third city was Verden, Utah.

He was wanted for questioning in the murder investigation of his ex-wife's husband. The ballistics in that murder case identified the murder weapon as a .357 Ruger

> *"He was wanted for questioning in the murder investigation of his ex-wife's husband."*

Blackhawk. The Verdan, Utah police department also had an inquiry from

Watson Lakes, Canada for a background check due to his application to work in the Wildlife and Forest Department.

When Terry called me with all this information both our minds began to turn in the same direction.

My first thought was, $5000 for repossessing cars? I found out the going rate was about $125 - $150 per car. That would be 30-40 cars, which would take weeks and months to track down and recover that many cars to make $5000.

Then it hit me. That's the same amount the ex con told Barry it would cost him to fill a contract on someone.

No wonder Barry told the police he gave $5000 to my dad to cover the payroll. That would justify the missing $5000. A burglar must have surprised dad and shot him. Yeah, right!

Barry had no idea; he was about to have to pay for what he did!

MURDER FOR HIRE

CHAPTER SEVEN: The Package

MURDER FOR HIRE

CHAPTER SEVEN: The Package

When Terry Jordan informed the director of the homicide division about the findings in Kansas, he was instructed to get the package put on the next flight to Oklahoma City.

When it arrived, they were stunned when they opened the package and saw the contents: a .357 Ruger Blackhawk, automatic weapon. The serial number was filed off as expected and there were no fingerprints.

Sgt. Jordan immediately notified the Utah Police department since the murder weapon in their case was a .357 Ruger Blackhawk. They requested it be sent over night so they could run ballistics to compare with the recovered rounds in their case.

He informed them it would not be possible to oblige their request until after the revolver was sent to the FBI for ballistics in this case.

This was huge and definitely not a coincidence, especially if it was the murder weapon in the Utah case.

But where is this John Blake?

The wait for the ballistics test from the FBI made every day seem longer.

The next day Terry called me and asked me to go with him to the last known address of John Blake. He wasn't sure who lived there now, but it still listed John Blake's mother, Edith Blake. Terry showed me the address and I was surprised how close it was in proximity to my father's business. It was across the freeway and only eight blocks to the west.

Sgt Jordan wanted to get a current picture to show Donna Miller from the nightclub and find out if John Blake's' mother knew he was in town the week of February 5th.

Why did he stay in a motel?

When Terry knocked on the door, a lady came to the door that seemed to be in her mid 50's. He identified himself as a sergeant with the police department and John Blake had applied as a Forest Ranger in Canada. There was a background inquiry that required some family information and a current picture if possible.

The lady explained that Mrs. Blake was at her church cooking for a church function.

Her next words took my breath. She said, "Edith's sister, Marilyn Tindale, is here. Maybe she can answer your questions." I stepped away from the door so I couldn't be seen and whispered to Terry, " That's Barry's wife!"

Oh my gosh! My mind was swirling as I'm leaning up against the doorframe to keep Marilyn from seeing me. Sgt. Jordan explained the background information request from Canadian authorities and Marilyn said she didn't know much about John Blake since he was a nephew and had been gone a long time.

He then asked what church Edith Blake worked at and we left hurriedly.
We sat in the car and updated what we had so far.

First, my dad's partner comes to the crime scene with an attorney and is slow to answer any questions and not be cooperative with the police.

Second, he cleans the crime scene of blood inside the crime scene tape and opens the doors for business as usual as if nothing had happened the night before.

Third, two teen girls, walking across the parking lot of the business forty-five minutes before the time of my father's death, identify the partner waiting in his car.

Fourth, two ex cons identify Barry Tindale as the man who inquired about the cost of a contract to kill.

Fifth, the man that registered at a motel just down the street from my father's home, registered under an assumed name of Jack Steele (who actually owed the business a huge amount of money), met with Barry Tindale the night before my father was killed. Steele made two phone calls to two women he was having an affair with and was identified as John Blake, not Jack Steele, then sent one of them a gun when he couldn't cross into Canada, then lied to both of them about what he was doing in Oklahoma City. Then he used the address of Barry's parents-in-law from another state when he registered. And was also Barry's nephew.

WOW! It's coming together. We were ready to go see Mrs. Blake.

We pulled up to the church, went inside to ask for Mrs. Blake. They directed us to the kitchen in the basement.

When we walked into the kitchen, there was the sweetest looking grandmother. We introduced ourselves and she said, "Oh no, what's John done now?" Sgt Jordan explained the background check again, but did not mention John as a suspect in this investigation.

She explained that John had been adopted and had caused her heartache since he was a young boy. She said I don't think at my age I could take any more pain from his wild lifestyle. Sgt. Jordan asked her when she had spoken to or seen John the last time. She said it had been years, probably seven or eight. He said, "You didn't speak to him in February of this year?" She said, "No."

> "She said I don't think at my age I could take any more pain from his wild lifestyle."

Terry didn't have the heart to tell this sweet lady that her stepson, John, had been in town and hadn't even called her. That's not normal for a son, even adopted sons to not stay in touch with their mother.

Sgt. Jordan asked Mrs. Blake if she had a recent photograph of John. She said she had one but it was not recent. She gave us a photo from her purse and he promised to return it to her within the week.

It's beginning to look like Barry hired his nephew, John Blake to kill my dad. That had to be why it happened so quick after my dad gave Barry the first option to buy him out. Three weeks later my dad is murdered, so Barry could get the business and not have to go through an audit or pay to buy out my dad's half of the business. Yes, they had a buy/sell agreement that if a partner died, his wife got $75,000. But that was nothing compared to what the business was really worth.

I was at the point now that I would just as soon have Barry Tindale prosecuted than the actual contract killer, even if Barry didn't actually kill him.

It presented a dilemma to the police and the prosecutors at the district attorney's office. They could find no trace of John Blake anywhere. An arrest warrant was issued for him, but there had been no response, even with the reward we were offering.

But it did not present a dilemma to me. Barry would work just fine as far as I was concerned, even if we never found John Blake.

Barry's the one that had murder in his heart and was going to pay for what he did!

MURDER FOR HIRE

CHAPTER EIGHT: THE REWARD

MURDER FOR HIRE

CHAPTER EIGHT: THE REWARD

Finally, after eight months, we got the results back from the FBI ballistics lab. The report said the rounds were too damaged to define the grooves and markings on the actual bullets retrieved at the scene. But they were able to determine the type of revolver that was used.

A .357 Ruger, Blackhawk. Exactly the same type of revolver that was in the package John Blake had sent his mistress in Kansas. The report did reveal one other thing. The Utah police had requested the FBI lab run ballistics for their case with this same revolver. Bingo! It was a match. So the man that Barry met at the nightclub the evening before my father was killed had mailed the murder weapon in the Utah case to his girlfriend in Kansas.

I asked Terry how much that would help us in the evidence. He said it's just another piece of the puzzle and assured me we were on the right trail but needed more concrete evidence.

It was now about ten months into the investigation and I wanted to see charges filed against Barry and a trial to begin soon. The detectives or the District Attorneys office never seemed to be in as big a hurry as I was to put more pressure on Barry and force his hand and expose himself.
I knew then I needed to get more involved in Barry's daily life.

I began to spend my days following him as he headed out each morning.

I would wait at a convenience store just a few blocks from his house. It was the only way out of his neighborhood and the entrance to the expressway that took him to his business.

He never seemed to notice me as I followed him to the office and various errands he ran during the day.

One particular day he met a woman for lunch at a club downtown. It was open for lunch and drinks at 11 am each day during the week. It was also very dark inside and seemed a peculiar setting for a business lunch.

It became obvious after a few weeks of lunch meetings with the same woman that it was business all right, monkey business.
I got her license plate number and turned it over to Sergeant Jordan.
 He ran the plates and discovered the car was registered to a Ron and Judy Darnell. Sgt Jordan ran a background check, warrants, everything he could find out about them.

Surprisingly, there was nothing in their background check; everything came out clean as a whistle, except she was seeing another married man, Barry Tindale!

After several months of a weekly rendezvous they came out of the club around 1:30pm and got in Barry's car and headed to a motel.

After he got a room, I took pictures of them getting out of his car and entering their room.

It was two hours before they came out and the pictures of them leaving the room together were perfect for what I had in mind.

I wasn't sure it meant anything to the homicide investigation. But I was sure of one thing. It would make utter turmoil for the married woman's husband and Barry's wife, Marilyn.

I knew somehow, someway I was going to make Barry pay for what he did. Either he would spend his life inside prison walls or I would make him feel imprisoned. Maybe, just maybe I could put enough pressure on him that mentally he would breakdown, or even commit suicide. And I would be guilty of nothing except fulfilling the vow I made to my father.

I developed the pictures and immediately sent them to Ron and Darnell Marilyn Tindale.

> "Either he would spend his life inside prison walls or I would make him feel imprisoned."

I even placed an anonymous call to Ron Darnell to let him know of the ongoing murder investigation that focused on Barry Tindale.

Ron begged me to tell him who I was but I told him I only wanted revenge for Barry Tindale. Ron told me he was having a subpoena issued for Barry to be a witness against his wife since she denied any involvement or knowing Barry.

Soon there was a divorce filing in the newspaper of Ron Darnell vs. Judy Darnell. I couldn't wait for the court date.

I made sure Marilyn Tindale knew her husband had been served a subpoena.

Somehow this all seemed to satisfy the hate and anger in my heart for this man.

I also wanted Barry to see me in the back of the courtroom. I wanted to totally intimidate him and put fear in him.

On the day of the divorce proceedings, Barry was sworn in and questioned on the witness stand.

Sure enough he denied everything and then Ron's attorney entered the pictures into evidence and the judge had Barry arrested for perjury.

I loved it! I left the courtroom with a satisfaction that this was just the beginning of Barry's life going down.

It seemed to me it was getting better and better as each day passed.

I had no idea that the hate and pain and revenge in my heart would drive me to the edge of almost committing a worse tragedy than what we had already been through.

Barry began to spend more and more time after work drinking and frequenting bars and clubs late into the night, week after week.

It was during the next three months that he met a man at a club one night that opened up another arena of interest.
I got his license plate and turned it over to Sgt. Jordan.
His name was Albert DeMarco and he was involved in politics and had been a campaign manager for numerous other candidates for the House of Representatives and Senate positions at the state level.
Sergeant Jordan felt it was necessary to interview this man personally.
Much to our surprise, Barry Tindale was about to run for the House of Representatives.
At this point I contacted Mr. DeMarco and made sure he knew Barry's background of adultery and as much of the murder investigation that Sgt Jordan would let me reveal to him.

The next week, Mr. DeMarco resigned as his campaign manager and Barry withdrew his name from the political arena.

Truly Barry was crazy. How could he even have a thought of such a position with him just perjuring himself a few months earlier? Besides the fact he was the prime suspect of an ongoing murder investigation of his business partner.

I made sure that the newspaper articles were always slanted toward Barry as the prime suspect. I was not going to let up now. I wanted to be as relentless and tenacious as legally possible so justice would be served for my father.

I followed him one day and he pulled into a church where a funeral was about to begin.

I waited for him to go inside and went inside and sat right behind him. I leaned forward and whispered in his ear, " I know and you know and you're going to pay for what you did. Over and over I kept repeating the same thing to him. Finally he got out of the pew and hurried to the men's room holding his hand over his mouth. I got up and followed him like a concerned friend. When I went in the bathroom he was down on his knees in a stall, throwing up. I kicked open the stall door, opened my coat so he could see the two guns and said, " I know and you know." I was hoping I could drive him to suicide.

The night Barry withdrew from his political aspirations he went to his favorite drinking spot. After three hours of non stop drinking he came out obviously very drunk and got in his car.

I followed him onto the expressway as he weaved across the highway lanes from one side to the other.

I'm not sure what came over me but I thought if I could get him to run into my van it would be another way to keep him backed into a corner and having to face me for one more thing in his life.

We were approaching a sharp curve and he was in the inside lane. I accelerated to get in front of him and slammed on my brakes to make him rear end me, he over reacted. He jerked his steering wheel to the left, over steered his car and lost control and went through the guardrail. His car rolled over and over down an embankment several times. It scared me for a moment because I thought I truly had killed him. I pulled onto the shoulder as his car came to a rest.

Next thing I know, Barry had crawled out of his car and was walking around. I called 911 and told them a car went through a guardrail and down an embankment at the Hillsboro exit of the main expressway in town. I was hoping the city would charge him with destroying public property since he went through 50 feet of guardrail.
Even though the reward ads had not produced much results, it felt like I was getting a different kind of reward.

I'm not going to let up or back away.

MURDER FOR HIRE

CHAPTER NINE: What The Hell?

MURDER FOR HIRE

CHAPTER NINE: What The Hell?

By this time the homicide detectives believed the only thing left to pursue was auditing the books of Barry's business to confirm what my dad had suspected.

That was going to be my dad's next move. Audit the books to get things out in the open once and for all. Dad wouldn't be able to sell his share of the business without an audit to assure the buyer of his investment. My mother and I both had informed the detectives of the issues between Barry and my dad.

Dad felt all along Barry was covering something up in the books. I'm not sure what or why dad didn't understand their financial statements although he continually suspected Barry of pilfering. The business never had enough money to pay all their bills on a timely basis. Nor were they able to meet the entire payroll twice a month without holding their own checks for a few days. Cash flow was a problem although sales were up each quarter. Account receivables didn't seem to be delinquent enough to cause the severity of never having enough.

But one thing dad knew was that Barry was very protective of the books and constantly took them home nightly and kept everything under lock and key.

The homicide division believed an audit might reveal enough to show motive and file charges. I'm not sure how Barry got wind of the audit but when the detectives subpoenaed the company's books, they weren't available. The legal maneuvering had begun. Barry's attorney filed an injunction to stop the court order from securing their books.

I'm not sure I ever got a clear answer as to the legal ground they took but it stopped the subpoena.

In the meantime, the assistant district attorney, Steven Hill, requested a meeting with Ray Hart, the head of the homicide division.

They reviewed all the evidence in the case and the assistant D.A. said he would take it to the District Attorney (Frank Wallis). He made a statement to Ray Hart that astounded me. He said, "You know Frank is going to run for State

> "He is not going to want to file charges against anyone that isn't going to be an iron clad case."

Attorney General?" Ray Hart responded with, "What difference does that make?" Steven said, " Any case he prosecutes between now and the elections will either be a feather in his cap or a mark against his campaign. He is not going to want to file charges against anyone that isn't going to be an iron clad case."

Ray was shocked that the political future of this man might be the deciding factor of whether a murderer would go free or be pursued in the judicial system.

When Ray got back to the police department he called Terry Jordan into his office and made him aware of some political maneuvering that might influence the outcome of this case.

It was going to be difficult for Terry not to tell me. We had spent an incredible amount of time together over the past eighteen months and probably knew each other as good as most of the members of his homicide division. We had talked about the things I was going through especially with my mom, who had been in almost a vegetative state. She was under a doctor's care; trying to deal with her life now. Not being able to bring closure to dad's death was unbearable for her.

I realized that if dad had been killed in a car wreck or some other way, it would have been easier to move forward with our lives. But day in and day out there was a constant reminder of the brutality of this murder. It was going on almost two years now and it seemed like it was not a priority now within the homicide division.

Since my father had been murdered, there were nine other homicides in the next eleven months. Terry explained the difficulties the detective division faced with the added workload, while working all the old cases and the toll it took on them mentally and personally with their families. Not only were the crime scenes so difficult to deal with but the judicial system seemed to be protecting the suspects more than the victims.

When Terry finally told me about this political, bureaucratic crap. I was incensed. I could only say, "WHAT THE HELL? "

Don't even tell me there is a possibility that this case won't be tried and the man that

murdered or had him murdered will not have to pay for what he did.
WHERE'S THE JUSTICE?
What good is the judicial system if it's not going to bring justice?

I was not going to stand for this!

They better not even think about not filing charges against him. I was willing to use every last dime and every last breath to bring my father's murderer to justice.

Barry is going to pay for what he did!

MURDER FOR HIRE

CHAPTER TEN: The Trial

Murder For Hire

CHAPTER TEN: The Trial

FINALLY! Charges were filed!

Barry was arrested, arraigned and posted bond. The charges were first-degree murder and conspiracy to commit murder.

The DA's office hoped that Barry would plead states evidence and plea bargain to a lesser charge by exposing his nephew as the one who actually killed my father.

But once he did that, he would be admitting his part in the conspiracy to commit murder. That would also get him life at least with an outside chance of the death penalty. It never got close to a plea deal.

He wanted to go all the way, believing he would get a not guilty verdict and walk away a free man from all charges. There was no way with all the evidence pointing to him that he would get away with murdering my dad or at least the charge of hiring a contract killer.

I still felt that Barry was the real one with murder in his heart. Even if he didn't actually pull the trigger, he planned it. He was the cause behind my fathers' demise. A contract killer? It was just a job. It's impersonal to him. Yes, it was cold hearted but he didn't have anything personal against my dad. He didn't even know him. Barry did!

Finally we were going to get justice!

The jury selection was the beginning of an eye opening experience. Each side, the prosecution and the defense attorney had so many selections and deletions (or dismissals) in order to end up with a fair and impartial jury. But it seemed like the defense attorney was only interested in people who seemed unfair and partial.

Listening to the judges' instructions to the jury became an eye opening experience.

I couldn't believe the emphasis was not on the overwhelming evidence or that truth would be brought out in the open. But that the burden of proof was on the

> *"Day by day I listened to the defense attorney tear apart the evidence and create reasonable doubt."*

prosecution to bring testimony, evidence and proof that would leave no room for doubt.

Reasonable doubt was the exact words.

The prosecuting attorneys began calling their witnesses. It didn't take long to see the focus of the defense attorney. He only had to bring or raise reasonable doubt in the jurors' minds. He didn't have to prove anything. What is reasonable doubt versus unreasonable doubt? That's where the fine line is in our legal system. I know that no system is flawless but nothing seems fair when you're not getting justice and the perpetrator is not going to have to pay for what they did.

Day by day I listened to the defense attorney tear apart the evidence and create reasonable doubt.
The first witness was the police dispatcher that called the home of Barry Tindale to notify him of his partners' death. The attorney introduced the audio recording of the phone call.

When Marilyn Tindale answered the phone. The dispatcher asked if Barry Tindale was home. Her response was, "yes, he just walked in." Even though Barry denied, he "just walked in" and stated he got home at 7pm and never left until the call from police.

When it was the defense's turn to cross examined the dispatcher, he asked if his interpretation of Mrs. Tindale's response on the phone seemed as if she was saying Barry had just walked in the room or had just got home. He said," I didn't think either way."
That wasn't any help.

The prosecutors and the homicide detectives knew different, since he had been identified parked behind the business at 9pm the night of the murder. When Barry was questioned at the crime scene of his whereabouts earlier that night, he told the police he had been home since 7pm.

The next witness was Donna Miller from the nightclub. She saw Barry Tindale and Jack Steele (who was later identified as John Blake) meet at her club. She testified as to the date and time the two men met the night before the murder. She had given a description of this 'Jack Steele" and the artists sketch was introduced at that time.

Even though the picture retrieved from John Blake's mother was 15 years old it was introduced also and both sketch and the picture looked like the same man. Donna Miller identified John Blake as the "Jack Steele" who met with Barry on February 4th.

The prosecution brought out the entire scenario tying Barry Tindale to every aspect of the trail of evidence along with the address of this Jack Steele from the hotel that belonged to Barry's in-laws in Ohio.

Next witness was Sergeant Terry Jordan, lead detective on this case.
The prosecutors questions were short and to the point and involved an overview of how the entire murder was planned and controlled within the confines of Barry's family. From using his mother in laws address on a bogus hotel registration to meeting his nephew in a nightclub the night before the murder. The nephew being the same person that would probably be convicted of murder in Utah if he was ever

located. All evidence followed a trail back to Barry Tindale.

The defense attorneys' questions were not short and sweet. There were about standard operating procedure for a witness photograph identification of a suspect?

He asked Terry if two to three pictures of other men with similar physical characteristics in a similar car under similar lighting were shown, to the two female witnesses along with the picture of Barry Tindale.
Terry responded, "No." Then Barry's attorney asked what each girl was shown when they came to the police station. Terry said, " a picture of Barry Tindale."
The defense attorney said the girls had no opportunity to see the similarity of physical facial features of other men at night with parking lot lighting. He emphasized that anyone with similar looks in poor lighting could have been identified as Barry Tindale if they were shown one picture. Terry said, yes. They would never know if the girls

would have picked Barry's picture with other pictures of men in similar settings.
That's reasonable doubt about the witness's identification of Barry.

Next witnesses were the two girls who identified Barry Tindale sitting in his car approximately 9pm behind his business.
Again the prosecutor had them testify, one after the other. They brought in the first girl; she testified then they brought in the second girl.

They both basically said the same thing as to the time he was sitting in his car, his description and the make of car he was driving, which was a match to his very own personal car. Their testimony further collaborated the time spectrum of the "Security Patrol' phone call to my dad, 9pm on February 4th. The estimated time of death, 9:40pm and the estimated time of Barry's return to home, 10:45pm.

The cross-examination of each girl attacked her identification of Barry as the man in the car behind the business.

Then he asked one of them a question that astounded everyone. Have you spoken to Barry Tindale since the night you identified him.

One said yes, and the other said no. The one girl, who said yes, stated that Barry Tindale had contacted her at the Black Castle café one night and asked her if she saw him in the parking lot the night of the murder. She was so scared she told him no. Barry's attorney asked her another question. "Did you tell the police?" She said, "No, I was too scared."
So did you see him or not the night of February 5th night? Yes, she said. Are you scared now? Are you telling the truth now? Are you hiding anything else from this court? The prosecutor objected and it was sustained. No further questions for this witness.

The defense attorney entered a motion to have the girls testimony removed since his client had contact with the prosecutors witness's.

The judge denied it and said move on.

Next witnesses were the two men with criminal records for burglary and dope dealing. They identified Barry Tindale as the person who asked them about what a contract would cost to kill someone.

Each man was asked how he knew the defendant. Their responses were similar in that they had done business with him before. Legal or illegal asked the prosecutor. Legal of course, each responded.
The prosecutor asked them to identify the man that contacted them and asked what it would cost to have someone killed. Both men, one after the other identified Barry Tindale as the man.

Now it was the defenses turn. The defense attorney bombarded them with questions about their criminal records. Then he badgered them with accusations of lies and whether they had made up stories about Barry in order to get reduced sentences on other criminal charges against them. His next question raised some eyebrows amongst the jurors.

How many people have asked you what it would cost to have someone killed. Each man said, "A bunch." Next question. Have you ever killed someone for money? "NO!" was their individual response. Same questions, same answers at two different times of testifying. It would have been better for the prosecution to have split up these two witnesses and had one testify one day and the other another day. But putting them on the stand right after each other seemed to be a big mistake.

All the defense had to do was raise, "reasonable doubt."

So far it seemed like the prosecutor had made the defense attorneys job easy. The next witness was Donna Miller, the bartender at the Saratoga Club.

The Assistant District attorney asked her relationship or knowledge of the deceased, Jack King. She said she knew Mr. King because she bought supplies from his company for the nightclub she worked.
He asked her if both partners in the business made sales calls, she said no.
She said my dad stopped by about once a week.

He asked her if my dad was ever in the club with anyone else or met anyone else, she said no. His next question was this. Has his partner ever been in your club? She said yes. He asked, how many times? She said, once. He asked if she remembered the date. She said, February 4th. He asked her how she remembered the date so vividly. She said, "Because it was the night before Mr. King was murdered."

He said tell us what you remember from that night: Barry Tindale met a man in the club around 7pm. She recognized him from when she had been in the store to buy supplies.

When she served their drinks she acknowledged him by name and he responded in a shocking manner. He said, how did you know my name? She told him she was in his business a few months ago and your partner introduced us. He did not seem happy that she recognized him.

Donna turned to the other man and introduced herself and asked him his name. The man stuttered and stammered and finally Barry said, his name is Jack Steele but he's from out of town. Donna said you must be staying in our motel and he said yes. She wrote his name on the bar tab so she could greet him by name if he was there the next night. The attorney asked if she ever saw him again, she said no. Once again, the defense attorney began to ask her questions of relevance. Was it unusual for businessmen to have business meetings in her club? She said no. Were you suspicious of Barry and this man on that night, she said no.

She tried to interject that later it was discovered that was not the man's name and the defense attorney objected. The judge directed the jurors to disregard her statement and for the court clerk to strike it from the records.

At that time the assistant district attorney entered the registration records into evidence. The agent from the Kansas Bureau of Investigation was called as the next witness. He read different parts from the report that revealed the man that had made calls from the room registered under the name of Jack Steele was actually John Blake, who was missing and was wanted in several states for questioning for murder and extortion. It contained the information about phone conversations two married women had with John Blake from the same motel on the same night of February 4th.

He had the signed affidavits from each woman about their phone conversations pertaining to what John Blake was doing and the amount of money he stated he was being paid, $5000.

He stated there was a package they recovered from one of the women's house that John Blake had sent her from the Canadian border. When asked what the contents of the package were, he stated, he didn't know. It was at this time the prosecution entered the .357 Ruger Blackhawk into evidence. The defense attorney objected as to relevance but the judge denied his objection.

The prosecutor had no more questions for this witness.

Now the defense attorney began his barrage of questions and courtroom shenanigans. He tried over and over to trip the Kansas Agent up in his report and asked why these two women weren't here on the witness stand. The agent said he could have them in the courtroom if needed.

Next witness for the prosecution was the bank manager of Dad and Barry's business. She was there to testify about business banking procedures and payroll processing. The prosecutor was going to connect the $5000 Barry said he gave to my dad to the testimony of the bank manager. His question to her pertained to her familiarity with the company's business account including the payroll.

She explained the constant monitoring of their cash flow in order to pay checks sometimes when there wasn't sufficient funds, thus over-drafting the operating account. Therefore all deposits were made in the operating account and in eleven years, week after week, money was transferred into the payroll account.

She testified they had never made a direct deposit into the payroll account like Barry said he had instructed my dad to do. She produced records that showed the largest cash deposit into the operating account was $600.

Deposits were 99% with customer checks. They just didn't deal with much cash at any given time. She testified of odd amounts of cash withdrawals from February 1st to 5th, $1118, $1276, $1193, $1012 and $401

for a total of $5000. It was just one more piece of the puzzle fitting quite nicely.

The defense attorney asked how many other businesses required personal attention with their operating accounts and their payroll. She said, too numerous to count.

His next question seemed to take the wind out of her testimony. He asked if this was a true statement, "is it normal or standard operating procedure to offer this same service and attention to all your banking customers?" She said yes.

No more questions!

The Asst. DA recalled Sgt Jordan to the witness stand. He asked him to read the report from the Utah homicide investigation. The report identified the .357 Ruger Blackhawk that had been sent to the woman in Kansas from John Blake as the murder weapon in their homicide case.
The prosecutor retraced the trail of the revolver and the evidence Sgt Jordan had gathered against Barry Tindale.

The FBI's ballistic tests were presented. Even though the tests were inconclusive as to whether they were fired out of this same gun. The FBI said the rounds that were tested had enough markings on them to identify the murder weapon as a .357 Ruger Blackhawk. The prosecution rested.

The defense had no witnesses and certainly was not going to put Barry Tindale on the stand.

They stood on the 'reasonable doubt" they were confidant they had raised with every witness.
The next day would be closing statements for each side.

Hey Barry, tomorrow is your last day of freedom.

MURDER FOR HIRE

CHAPTER ELEVEN: The Verdict

MURDER FOR HIRE

CHAPTER ELEVEN: The Verdict

I guess that night was the first night I talked to God since I blamed him for letting my dad get murdered. I asked God to make sure the jury convicted Barry Tindale based on the truth that every witness had testified. I said, "God, that's what justice is suppose to be about, Truth!"

When court convened, it was February 4th, almost two years to the day that my father was killed. I knew there would be poetic justice. We had waited so long for this day.

> "I knew there would be poetic justice. We had waited so long for this day."

The prosecution made their closing statements. It took an hour to review the testimony and relate everything to the jury they heard over the past several days. The assistant D.A. said there is only one person that had motive, opportunity and the right acquaintances to pull this off.

The jury listened intently and was commanded to bring back a guilty verdict for the sake of justice and truth that came from every witness. He told them, don't ignore the truth just because the defense is experienced at manipulating people's testimonies.

It was the defense attorneys' turn now. He stated that the prosecutor had done nothing except present a lot of circumstantial evidence.
None of it was concrete or conclusive. The gun that was produced was not proven to be the murder weapon. As sophisticated as the FBI's ballistics labs were, they didn't prove the rounds were fired from this gun.

He said the detectives couldn't even find this "phantom nephew." They could only produce two scared teenage girls. Two ex-cons trying to plead for shorter time on other charges to help out the prosecutions case.

They produced a nightclub manager that served drinks to two men having a drink and a bank manager that spends all her time over drafting accounts for incompetent business managers.

He told them there wasn't reasonable doubt in this case, but that there was no doubt they had the completely wrong man and did not prove anything against his client. His last statement was, "There is no murderer in this room unless you find him guilty, and then you're the murderer. He is not guilty and each one of you know it in your heart and mind."

I was infuriated and worried, but I knew God would bring vengeance on Barry.

The jury was out all day and finally had a verdict at 4pm. At 4:15pm on February 4th the judge read the jurors decision, then handed it back to the court clerk.

Then the judge said, " In the charge of first degree murder, how do you find the defendant? Not Guilty. In the second charge of conspiracy to commit murder, how do you find the defendant, Not Guilty, they stated."

Unbelievable! No way! This isn't happening! I had never felt so much rage and despair. I was angry with the defense attorney, the jury, the judge and Barry!

I went over to Barry, as he was being congratulated and looked him in the face and said, *"I know and you know and you're going to pay for what you did!"*

Sgt. Jordan grabbed me and drug me out of the courtroom.

Barry's attorney went immediately and filed for a restraining order against me.

One of the detectives outside the courtroom was as infuriated as I was. He called me to the side and said, "Jack, the only way there will ever be any justice in your dad's case is to take Barry to Johnson County and shoot him with a shotgun." I said, "really? Why a shotgun? He said, because you can't trace a shotgun. I thought, hmmmmm, I like that, and if Barry can get away with murder, so can I. Then I asked him, why Johnson county? He said, "They've never solved a homicide!" I laughed, he laughed but it dropped deep into my heart and every day after that when the hate and anger and revenge would rise up inside me, I would picture me blowing Barry away with a shotgun and it seemed to appease the pain in my heart.

I wanted him to pay and one last strategy to keep the pressure on was to bring civil charges against him with a grand jury.

That became my passion now, collecting signatures on a grand jury petition. I learned from one of the assistant district attorneys to find another reason for the grand jury that might only take a few hours or one day then slip my dad's case on them without Barry and his legal hounds having any advance notice to prepare.

There was a small town in our county that I knew the chief of police and he had told me there were some misappropriations of funds with the city manager.

This was perfect; I was not going to give up.

But my friend David had other plans for me and I guess God did too.

Murder For Hire

CHAPTER TWELVE:
How Are You Doing Jack?

CHAPTER TWELVE:
How Are You Doing Jack?

This might amaze you after reading everything so far, but I was raised in church. It's not like I didn't know right from wrong. I guess when something this tragic happens in your life, your real character comes forth. My military background as a United States Army Drill Sergeant gave me a "kick butt, take names, ask questions later" mentality. But the church I was raised in, all I remember was we were supposed to be loving and caring and that was what it took to be a Christian. I thought I was a Christian. I tried to be a good husband and a good father. I tried to be a loving and caring man. But I realized later if I had died I would have gone to hell.

All during this period in my life, I had one friend (David Miller) that would keep checking with me constantly. He would always ask me, how are you doing? I would respond with the latest investigative details.

He would respond by saying, no Jack, How are YOU doing? I didn't want to talk about how I was doing. My identification, my goal, my purpose in life was to fulfill my vow to my dad. He was a true friend. The men in my church never reached out to me in any way. Not one man knew what to say. I know

> "I guess when men don't know what to say or do; they don't do or say anything."

I was full of hate and anger and revenge and was probably unreachable at this moment in my life. But I didn't understand why it seemed none of the men cared. I guess when men don't know what to say or do; they don't do or say anything. That shows they really weren't my friends.

But my friend David cared. He asked me if I had ever mourned my father's death.

I said, "What do you mean?" He said, "I never saw you shed one tear at your father's funeral."

He told me, "Mourning is God's way of helping you move on with your life. If you don't mourn and grieve your loved ones death then you are still living in the past with them."

He said, "Get in my car and come with me." I asked him where we were going, he said, "just trust me." He was the one man in my life that I totally trusted.

We pulled into the cemetery where my father was buried. I had no idea what he was doing or why we were there.

We walked over to my fathers' grave and he said, "Tell him good-bye." Lie down on your father's grave and tell him good-bye. I wasn't sure I could do this. It was too overwhelming. I thought about those words. So I said, "What?" David said it again, "Tell your dad good-bye." I didn't want to say good-bye until I could tell my dad, "We got your killer, I promised you I would get him." This was tough. It was like I was giving up. I wasn't ready to tell him good-bye.

I got down on one knee then laid face down and said it out loud, "Good bye Dad."

A flood of tears came rushing from my eyes and flooding down my face. I began to deeply sob and weep. I'm not sure how long I cried, seemed like 30 minutes, but was probably 2 minutes.

But something happened as I sat up. Something was different inside my chest. Everyday it felt like there was a rock or big knot under my chest, beside my heart. But now it was gone. The lump left, the knot was gone. How did that happen? It felt like 100 pounds had been lifted off my shoulders and chest. I never realized the relief that takes place in a person's life when they allow God's process to mourn and grieve their loved ones departure. I stood to my feet looked at him and he gave me the biggest hug and I began to cry again. I was thinking, what is up with all this crying, ball-baby! Be a man! I guess I was finally being a man.

But as I thought about it, it seemed as if I was getting a father's reassuring hug that everything was going to be all right.

We drove back to where my car was parked and as I reached to open the car door, he grasped my arm and said "I need to tell you one more thing...Jack, you're so full of hate and anger and revenge, you're going to end up causing a worse tragedy than what you have been through."

The words he spoke pierced my heart. It hurt to hear them but I knew they were true.

I didn't have a response. But I knew he loved me or he wouldn't be so concerned about me.

That night my family was sitting at the dinner table and we heard car tires squealing and heard our poodle, Brandy, yelping. I jumped up and ran out the front door and a silver corvette was racing up the street. Brandy was lying in the street with blood running out of his mouth. Our oldest daughter, Melissa, came out the door behind me. When she saw his limp body in the street she got on her knees trying to console Brandy but it was too late. She was crying and looking up at me in desperation for help. His lower body from his abdomen down was crushed.

Dads are supposed to be able to fix anything, especially for daddy's little girl. This was something I knew Daddy couldn't fix. The hurt in my daughters' eyes matched the pain in my heart that would not change the circumstances.

Suddenly, the same deep pain I felt the night my dad was murdered, was back. I jumped in our car and sped up the street catching the corvette at a stop sign several blocks way. I pulled in front of him to block him from taking off and slammed on my brakes. It reminded me of one of those Starsky and Hutch slides as my car slid sideways. I jumped out and had every intention of pulling him out of his car and beating him within an inch of his life. But when I got close, he had a shotgun pointing out his window at me and I said, "no beef" and backed up to my van. The driver took off. I was stunned and realized my anger, my pain, my heartache, my revenge was just looking for anybody to take it out on.

What is wrong with me? I had almost caused another tragedy. I could have been blown away with that shotgun. David was right. But he was concerned I would take the law in my hands to bring justice in my dad's case. I called him the next morning to tell him what happened and asked him if we could meet. We met and he asked me to go to a meeting with him. I agreed.

When I went to this meeting I heard the speaker say, "You can't understand how great God's love is until you understand how much you've been forgiven." And he said, "If there's just one man here tonight, that for the first time in your life you understand how much God loves you because of how much He's forgiven you, then I want to pray for you to settle things in your life." I knew I needed to get some things settled in my life.

For two years I had totally checked out. I was worn out and disgusted with myself.

I went forward and I fell on my knees...cried out to God and asked for forgiveness for my sins, my hate, my anger, the murder in my heart and accepted Jesus Christ as my Lord and Savior. When I stood up, the most incredible thing happened. Every bit of hate, every bit of anger, every bit of revenge was gone out of my heart! Explain that! How does God take hate, anger, bitterness, hurt and pain out of your heart? Is there a switch in there? Is there something He just reaches in and clicks a switch and it's gone? I don't know, but here's what I do know. I know that I know that I know that I know that I know that God changed my heart. In an instant He changed my life! I had no more desire to pursue my fathers' case. It was unbelievable! Almost too good to be true, but it was true!

Now what do I do?

I had such mixed feelings and emotions.

MURDER FOR HIRE

CHAPTER THIRTEEN:
Ed Cole Saved My life

MURDER FOR HIRE

CHAPTER THIRTEEN:
Ed Cole Saved My life

A few months later my friend David, called again to check on me and said, "Hey, there's a guy in town named Edwin Louis Cole who's doing a men's meeting. Why don't you go with me?" I said, "Alright."

His entire message was about forgiveness. I knew I needed to forgive my dad's partner. Ed Cole was telling the men that this was a crucial moment in the life of Christ because it was after Jesus was resurrected, but before He ascended to heaven. It's significant that He chose to speak to his disciples one last time about forgiveness. The scripture is John 20:22. The 22nd verse:

"And when he has said this, He breathed on them, and saith unto

them, Receive ye the Holy Ghost. Whosoever sins ye remit, they are remitted unto them; and whosesoever sins ye retain, they are retained."

Whosoever...that means somebody else. He said whosoever sins. Who's sins is He talking about here? Is He talking about their sins? No. He's talking about whosoever sins you remit. Whoever sins against you. Someone else's sins, not yours, whosoever sins you remit. Remit means release and release means forgive. When someone else sins against you, whosoever sins you remit, release or forgive, He says they are remitted, they are released, they are forgiven...but... whosoever sins you retain, they are retained. When someone else sins against you, when you forgive them, their sin is out of your life. You're free from what they did to you. You no longer carry their sin. You move on. You chose to not take offense. You choose to not let that rule and reign in your heart. You choose to not let that have control over your life. You chose to not let that offense have a greater influence in your heart and your life than the word of God and the love of God. It's our choice!

That's why the greatest power God has given us is the power of choice. He gave us a will. He didn't have to give us a will. It means much more to God when we chose for His will to be done, not our will. That's why we pray thy will be done, thy kingdom come on earth as it is in heaven" in the Lords prayer.

Now what does retain mean? Retain means retain. You have it. It's yours. You take it everywhere you go. You go to bed with it...get up with it. You go to work with it. You make love with it. You go to church with it. You retain it...until you release it. And how do you release it? By saying it with your mouth. You say it with your mouth and believe it in your heart. You say, I forgive you.

Brother Cole made an invitation to the men. He said, if you have someone you need to forgive, come down to this altar and let me pray with you.

I was the first of about 200 men that went forward to forgive someone.

He led us in a confession. He said you are only committed to what you confess. So confess with your mouth that you forgive that one who wronged you.

I said, "I forgive you Barry."

It was incredible.

I couldn't explain but once again I knew God had changed my heart.

I felt free for the first time in years. I also knew I could stand before God with no unforgiveness in my heart.

After he prayed for each man, I turned around to go back to my seat, and when I put my foot on the first step to go back to my seat, a voice spoke to my heart and said, "Now, you go to Barry and ask *him* to forgive you!" I knew it had to be God. I looked up at heaven and said, "Let me get this right God...I go to my dad's partner and tell him I forgive him..." He said, "No. You go to him and you ask him to forgive you." I said, "I'm sorry, God, I can't. What you're asking me to do is humanly impossible." He said, "Good. My grace will be sufficient." I thought, "What?" I didn't know what that meant. I didn't even know it was in the Bible. I went to my seat and my friend, David, was sitting there and he said, "Are you okay?" And I said, "Nope!" He said, "Why?" I told him what God had just spoke to my heart. That God had said, "Good, His grace would be sufficient."

I don't understand what that means." Dave said, "Oh Jack, that's simple. It's not until you and I finally admit we can't. It's then and only then that His grace can be the greatest strength in our life. As long as you think you can, Jack, it's by your might, it's by your power, it's by your strength, and not by His Spirit." I said, "Well, I tell you what, David, if this is going to happen in my life, it's going to have to be God!" Because I wasn't interested.

I left and went home. I didn't say anything to Betty about what had happened. I was afraid once again of what God wanted to do in my life.

My wife and I and our children had begun to pray in the mornings. We would gather in a circle and pray before the kids went to school. We would go around the circle and each one of them would pray, then Betty, the I would close in prayer.

That next morning, I was getting ready to close the prayer and say, "...in Jesus Name, amen." And just as I was getting ready to say, "...in Jesus Name..." the Lord spoke to my heart and said, "Pray for Barry!" I growled under my breath and hesitated for a long time and finally said...bless Barry, amen." Betty said, "What?" I said, "Nothing'". The next morning, we go around the circle, the kids pray, Betty prays. Now it's my turn to close in prayer and I'm getting to the "in Jesus Name" real quick. Sure enough, the Lord says, "Pray for Barry"...every morning..."Pray for Barry"...every morning...nine months... "Pray for Barry".

Can I admit to you that the prayers I prayed I didn't mean? I had learned that to obey is better than sacrifice. I was praying out of obedience. I didn't mean them. I called them *flapjack prayers.* Did you ever see those cartoons, when you were a kid, and the cook, the chef was doing flapjack pancakes and they'd flip them up in the air...and inevitably one would stick to the ceiling.

I was hoping one of my prayers would stick to the ceiling and God might think I really meant them. But I didn't...until one Saturday morning, we joined hands and I prayed for the first time from my heart and not my head and I prayed for Barry's soul that he might be saved. The blood of Barry's life seemed to be on my hands now. And I began to tremble as to what God was about to do, because something had gone from my head to my heart, and I was afraid of it. I said, no God, don't do this.

Murder For Hire

CHAPTER FOURTEEN:
Somebody Did Pay

MURDER FOR HIRE

CHAPTER FOURTEEN: Somebody Did Pay

It was nine months to the day that God had been having me pray for Barry. That evening my wife said, "Jack, I need you to go down to Williams's Meat Market and get me five pounds of ground beef." I said, "Honey, it's 9:00pm on Saturday night and Safeway is two blocks down the street. William's Meat Market is two miles away." She said, "We're having our Family Minister's Luncheon tomorrow. I want to make a meatloaf. I want five pounds of quality ground beef from William's Meat Market." I had read *Maximized Manhood*, so I went.

Thank God the footsteps of a righteous man are ordered because Williams's Meat Market was the on the same street as my father's business that Barry now owned. I came to the intersection of Smithfield and Main Street. All I could think about was that was my father's business that his partner now owned lock, stock and barrel. It just wasn't right.

When I pulled up to that intersection, it was totally blocked off and barricaded with fire engines for a seven-alarm fire. Both buildings of the business had caught fire and the ladders were in the air and they were pouring water into the top of the buildings. The buildings were across the street from each other. I looked down the street and saw the flames and said, "Yes!" That's just what he deserves. It was a moment I wanted to enjoy but the Lord would not let me. The Lord spoke to my heart and said, "go to him, he's there, ask him to forgive you."

I may have been sitting at an intersection of two streets, but actually I was at the crossroads of obedience and rebellion.

It's really that simple in our lives, when you know to do right and you don't do it. It's sin.

And there I sat at that intersection. Whose will is going to be done? It truly was a choice I had to make, Obey or rebel. Who's controlling my life now, me or Christ in me? I backed away from the roadblock and went to Williams's Meat Market and got the ground beef.

I drove back to the business and parked the same place I parked the night I found my dad. I walked up the alley and out on the sidewalk and there Barry stood by himself.

They had already put the fire out in the building on this side of the street and had busted all the display windows out. There was a little bit of smoke still coming out the opening but flames were still coming out of the building across the street. .

I hadn't been able to figure out what words I would say to him when this moment happened. I had tried to figure out what will I say to him? How do I say it?

You know when you're getting ready to go into a meeting with somebody and you kind of go over the conversation mentally in your mind? You know, okay I'll say this and then he'll say that and then I'll... I mean I had tried and tried...what do I say to this man? God, help me! What do I do? Call him on the phone, "Hey, Barry, want to do lunch?" And now, here was the moment I had stayed awake asking God, How do I do this?

Here's how God did it. I stood beside him and looked across the street at the burning buildings with him and said, "What happened?" He said, "They caught on fire." I said, "How?" He said, "I don't know. The fire marshal said he would tell me as soon as he figured something out." And then he looked at me and fear came over him. He backed away and started stumbling. His knees got weak. His face turned ash gray and he was about to faint...and I grabbed him and put my arms around him to keep him from falling down. For the first time I was able to mouth the words that I hadn't been able to figure out.

And here's what I said. "God's changed my life. And I've come tonight to ask you if you can find it in your heart to forgive me of accusing you of being responsible for murdering my dad." He said, "Aw, you don't have to do that." I said, "Yeah, I do. I wanted you dead, Barry. I'm the one that ran you off the Expressway the night you came out of a club drunk. I'm the one that got with your campaign manager when you ran for the House of Representatives and caused him to resign and you had to withdraw out of the political race. I'm the one who told your wife about the affair you were having and took pictures of you coming out of a motel with her and caused your divorce. I was full of hate and anger and revenge. I wanted you dead." I said, "Will you forgive me?" He said, "Sure."

Well, my mind just went off! The audacity of this man, knowing what he did and he so flippantly says to me, "Sure." My mind went nuts. I mean, that's where the battlefield is. The Bible calls these thoughts the fiery darts of the wicked ones. The devil wants you to take just one of them and grasp onto it and meditate on it until it gets from your mind into heart. You let the hate and anger come back in when you continually think about it and then you want to act on it.

I was glad the Lord was with me because my mind was trying to take over my mouth.

> "I knew for the first time in my life, it was no longer I that was living, but Christ in me.."

I knew for the first time in my life, it was no longer I that was living, but Christ in me. I said, "Let me ask you a question Barry, if you died tonight, do you know where you would go?"

He said, 'heaven," I said, "Why?" He said, "Because I have gone to church for 20 years and taught Sunday school." I said, "What else?" He said, "What else is there?"

I said, "The Bible only says one thing," and I quoted Rom10: 9,10 Paul said, "If you believe in your heart and confess with your mouth that Jesus died for your sins and rose from the dead, you shall be saved." Have you ever done that? He said No. I took his hand and said, then we need to pray and settle it once and for all.

I thought we would stand on the sidewalk in front of all these fireman and pray. But Barry took my hand and we stepped through a big display window they had busted out. We walked about fifteen feet from where I had found my father murdered, and by the grace of God I was able to pray the *sinner's prayer* with him and he asked God to forgive him and gave his heart to Jesus Christ. Instantly, he and I began to weep and sob and we embraced. I don't know how long we stood there and cried in each other's arms. Truly, they were the sounds of forgiveness.

Once again, God had done something in my heart that I couldn't explain, but I did know this, God changed my heart.

After we prayed we talked about the church I attended for about 30 minutes and I hoped he would come with me sometime. I turned around and walked back down the alley, and on my way to the car I heard a voice say, "Now, you've got the

"Now, you've got the cleansing, and I can launch you in the direction I called you to go."

cleansing, and I can launch you in that direction I called you to go. One thing was holding me back from the next level God had for me. It was unforgiveness.

It was holding me back from going to work for Edwin Louis Cole in his worldwide ministry to men. For the next fifteen years I was honored to serve him as associate minister. That was one of many things God had planned for my life. None of which would have happened if I had continued the life I was living.

Unforgiveness was holding me back from fulfilling the call of God to begin Faithful Men Ministries five years ago. None of this would have been fulfilled in my life if not for the grace of God.

I found out that the cleansing I got was according to I John 1:9 that says, *"...if we confess our sins, God is faithful and just to forgive us and* (here's the greatest part) *cleanse us from all unrighteousness."* Every unrighteous thing that's been done. Every bit of pain, every bit of hurt, every bit of hate, every bit of anger...God cleanses it from you. He cleanses us from all unrighteousness.

Because, when I left that night...here's what happened. Here's what the cleansing power of God did. Here's what happens when God cleanses that unrighteousness. Somehow He takes the hurt from the memory. Somehow, He takes the hurt and the pain from the memory. You always have the memory, but the pain doesn't come back with it any more. That's the power of God, unexplainable but undeniable.

You may say, where's the justice in forgiveness. It seems so unfair.

The same thing applies in our lives. When you and I realize how much God loves us and the price Jesus Christ paid on Calvary for our sins, it takes those questions out of the picture for us. Does it seem fair now? Sure it does when it applies to us!

No matter what you have done or had done to you! Jesus Christ set you free on Calvary. Just receive it and draw on God's grace to be the greatest strength in your life.

Let me interject the practical side of what else happened that night.

After Barry and I prayed together and I headed home, it was about 11pm. I had been gone two hours to get the ground beef. I'm sure Betty was wondering what happened to me.

One of the things I had learned from Edwin Cole's teachings was this.

Don't preach at your children. Share what God is doing in your life. Share what God is speaking to your heart.

So when I walked in the house and called out to Betty, I told her, "Honey, the most wonderful thing has happened. Get the kids up and bring them to the living room. She brought them downstairs and had them sit on the couch.

She and I sat on the floor in front of them and shared what God had just done in my life. I told them God had required of me to go to the man that had their grandfather murdered and ask him for forgiveness. Ask him to forgive me. I didn't think I had done anything wrong. But I had done something wrong. I wanted him dead. I had murder in my heart. And tonight God's grace gave me the strength to ask that man for forgiveness then share Christ with him and he accepted

Jesus Christ as his savior and we prayed together. Tears were flowing as I opened my heart to the kids and they began to realize the greatness of God in our lives.

Can I tell you that when Melissa, our oldest daughter, went on her first missions' trip to Mexico? The church asked if one of the young people had a testimony to share. The sponsor chose Melissa to go to the platform and she shared about the power of forgiveness from the night we sat on the floor in our living room and her dad told her what God had done in his life.

Remember dads, don't preach at your children, share what God is doing in your life.

The next thing that happened proved whether I could really walk in forgiveness. Two days later, Marilyn Tindale called me. She said, "Jack, I never would have believed God would use you in Barry's life." I said, "Marilyn, neither would I."

She said Barry called her the night before and told her what happened with the fire at the business. But then told her something else happened. He told her, God changed his life. I was really rejoicing and so was Marilyn. Then she said," I want to ask you something Jack and if you say no I totally understand."

" Barry is going to have a triple bypass on Friday and I don't know anyone else to ask this, but will you go pray for Barry and his surgery." I said, yes! I didn't even have to think about it.

On Friday I headed to the hospital and arrived at his room as the orderlies were taking him to surgery. I stopped them and he looked up at me and said, "What are you doing here?" I said, " I came to pray for you and get you healed." I laid my hand on his chest and prayed this, "In Jesus name, by the blood of Jesus and the stripes of Jesus, you are healed, Amen." He said, "Thank you." I said, "You're welcome, but don't thank me, thank Jesus, if it weren't for Him, neither one of us would be here."

There was more truth to that than I realized when I said it, because if not for Jesus, he would probably be dead and I would be in prison.

My friend David was right, I almost caused a worst tragedy than what we had already been through.

I remembered Edwin Cole saying , "There's a difference between "Churchianity" and Christianity."
Now I understood.

You may be wondering how the surgery went? He came out fine and they only had to do one bypass not three.

As you have been reading these last few pages has God spoke to your heart about anyone who's wronged you and you know you need to forgive them, you need to release their sin out of your life? That unforgiveness is holding you back from the next thing God has for you. They may never say, "I'm sorry." That person may never come to you and say; "I repent."

You may think somebody needs to pay for what they did to you.

I thought the same thing, until I found out somebody did pay! His name is Jesus. He paid for every person's sin so we wouldn't have to pay. When He hung on the cross and said, *"Father, forgive them for they know not what they do."* He was not only asking for forgiveness for the Roman soldiers and the thieves who hung on the cross beside Him, but He was asking forgiveness for you and me and every person who would ever sin or wrong you … for all of mankind, for all the history of time. In that moment never has so much forgiveness taken place.

And never in one moment did God and Jesus Christ exercise so much faith. It takes faith to forgive, because the person who hurt you may never come to you and say, "I'm sorry." They may never say, "I repent."

They may never come to you and ask you to forgive them. But Jesus Christ did. He stood in their stead. He stood in the place of those who wronged you and said, "I'm sorry, forgive me." He bore their sins. And He did no wrong. When you and I walk in unforgiveness, we make ourselves greater that God. God's never walked in unforgiveness.

Maybe you've tried, you've come to that point where you say, "God, it's humanly impossible to forgive the way you forgive. I need your grace." I need faith to forgive. I'm going to ask you to pray this prayer with me. If there is someone you need to forgive, do it now through this prayer. Maybe that somebody that you need to forgive is you. Sometimes we are harder on our self than anyone else.

Pray this prayer and release your faith and be cleansed from the unrighteous thing that was done to you.

"Father...in Jesus Name...I come to you...a child of God...asking You...to forgive me...for walking in unforgiveness...I

release...other's sins...out of my life...I don't want to retain them...I forgive them...and I ask You to forgive me...as I forgive others...set me free...cleanse my heart...from all unrighteousness...and I'll praise You for it...all the days of my life...in Jesus' Name...amen!

Glory to God. You can make this declaration "Whom the Son sets free is free indeed."

If God will do what He did for me, He will do it for you.

Maybe you have been like I was, living one way at home, a different way at work and another way in church but never had a personal relationship with Jesus Christ, you can settle that now.

Here's God's promise.

Romans 10: 9-13 That if you confess with your mouth the Lord Jesus, and believe in your heart that God has raised him from the dead, you shall be saved.

Rom 10:10 For with the heart man believeth unto righteousness; and with the mouth confession is made unto salvation.

Rom 10:11 For the Scripture says, whosoever believeth on him shall not be ashamed.

Rom 10:12 For there is no difference between the Jew and the Greek: for the same Lord over all is rich unto all that call upon him.

Rom 10:13 For whosoever shall call upon the name of the Lord shall be saved.

Pray this prayer and settle it for all of eternity.

"Father, I come to you in the name of Jesus. I repent of my sins. I ask you to forgive me. I believe in my heart and am confessing with my mouth that Jesus died for my sins and God raised Him from the dead. I am calling upon the name of the Lord, therefore I am saved! In Jesus name. Amen!

Now rejoice that your name is written in the Lambs Book of Life!

God has a plan for your life. Get involved in a church. Get into relationship with those who will encourage you in the faith and walk with you no matter what.

I have writing another book on Forgiveness. It's titled the *Unnatural Act of Forgiveness.* It contains scriptural teachings on forgiveness that God has taught me over the years.

You can check our website to see when it's released, www.fm318.com along with many other current books that will help you in your walk with the Lord. If there is someone you know that you feel would benefit from reading this book then please pass it on to them and order another one for the next person God puts on your heart to reach out to with this powerful message of forgiveness.

Please write to me a testimony of what God did in your life through this book and mail it to:

Faithful Men Ministries
PO Box 612241
Dallas, TX 75261

Or email me at jking@fm318.com

About the Author

Jack & Betty King

Jack C King is Founder and President of Faithful Men Ministries based in Dallas, TX.
He served Edwin Louis Cole, author, speaker and minister to men for fifteen years.
He has been married to Betty for forty years. They have five children and seven grandchildren.
He has spoken to men in thirty-nine states and twenty-seven countries about real manhood.
He is currently writing an in-depth book on forgiveness. It will be titled, "The Unnatural Act of Forgiveness." For the release date of this book and other resources please visit:
WWW.FM318.COM

To inquire about speaking engagements by mail:
FM318
PO Box 612241
Dallas, TX 75261
Or email
support@fm318.com
Or call toll free
1-877-399-1047

Acknowledgements:

I want to thank the Lord Jesus Christ for allowing me the time on this earth to write this testimony to His glory.

I owe so much to my wife Betty for her devoted love and respect and forgiveness. She has loved me when I didn't deserve to be loved, forgiven me when I didn't deserve to be forgiven and respected me when I didn't deserve to be respected. Thank you for praying for me, I love you.

My daughters, sons, grand daughters and grandsons have supported, prayed and loved me in so many ways. Thank you

Melissa & Rodney, Jocelyn, Hannah, Kaitlin, Kara & Scott, Ethan, Emma, Evan, Amber & Jonathan, Zac & Krista, Taylor and last but not least, Chad, for whom God has incredible, plans.

Tony Rorie, thank you for being a good spiritual son. I couldn't have finished this without your encouragement and hard work.

Especially my Board of Directors, Guy, Mike, Doug and Rance, I love you all.

And thank you Edwin Louis Cole for laying your life down to further the cause of Christ in men's lives around the world. I wouldn't have been able to do this without the encouragement and support of your family. Most of this book is because of the influence Edwin Cole had in my life after I lost my dad.